Nightshade Publishing Anthology

The Willow Tree Swing

Xanna Renae | Sheela Kean
Kristen Bazen | Kathryn Reilly
Hannah Carter | Cortney Manning | Beka Gremikova
Anne J. Hill | Julia Skinner | Willow Whitehead

PRINT 979-8-9850823-2-6
EBOOK 979-8-9850823-3-3

The Willow Tree Swing

Other Works by Nightshade Publishing

Anthologies

Of Ink & Paper
Balloon Children
The House Built Between the Branches

Short Stories

To Ponder
The Giant's Blade

Novels

Down with the Prince
Magic Like Fire

STORIES

"The world is fairly studded and strewn with pennies cast broadside from a generous hand. But—and this is the point—who gets excited by a mere penny?"

Annie Dillard
Pilgrim at Tinker Creek - 1974

NATURAL
GREEN

Moss

Xanna Renae

It spread across
   my fingers as I lay
   wound up in roots
of nature's play
shielding my skin
from golden leaves
and brushing my hair
the wind in the trees
I knew the soil
befriended the pebble
my new home
in pasture's rubble
the fife and strings
make melody
as I become
a memory

In Bloom

Sheela Kean

Lizzie was tired. Tired of everything.

"Have you called the doctor lately?" Kara sighed on the other end of the phone.

"Right. Like that ever helps anything." Lizzie answered.

"Aren't they supposed to? It's like their entire job."

"You'd think."

"So you don't want to come with us to the movies then? It's my birthday weekend. We're supposed to be having nonstop fun, remember?"

"I know, but you don't need me third-wheeling tonight. You two go on. I'll be home and you can tell me about it in the morning."

"Fine, get your rest then. You know what we're doing tomorrow and you absolutely cannot bail on me. You promised!"

Saying goodbye, Lizzie dropped her phone into her bag and gathered her things. She'd stopped for a coffee after shopping, giving her a chance to rest her feet. She loved her friends, they always tried to include her in everything, but that was overwhelming. Sometimes she needed the space to be alone with her pain.

Lizzie was chronically ill and it wore her down quickly. Nothing seemed to help her when it got bad. The flare-ups could last weeks, making hope feel far away. It was one of those things you couldn't really explain to someone else without feeling like they're judging you. You could always see it in their faces. Kara and Paul knew this when she'd moved in with them. They'd taken it as an eccentric personality trait, though, instead of an actual condition.

So Kara had saved all of Lizzie's flaky moments up for the year and used them as leverage, making her promise to take part in a birthday hike.

"Seriously, a hike. Who considers that fun?" She muttered with an eyeroll.

She would need all the extra energy she could muster for it, unlike her friends. So she'd planned a night of cozy TV watching instead of going out. *Who needs crowded theaters? I've got a heated blanket and a pile of pillows at home.*

This was the worst idea in the history of bad ideas. The twinge in her hip was only the beginning, nobody would be prepared for the fallout.

"How much further do you think?" Lizzie asked, trying her best to sound something other than distressed. She wheezed, the stitch in her side aching as she walked with a hobbled gait.

"Not too far. We're more than halfway," Paul replied.

"It's going to be so worth it. The garden is supposed to be

gorgeous and there's an entire room you can go in filled with butterflies!" Kara called out.

Lizzie could feel the sweat pooling under her clothes, making her even more uncomfortable. By the time they arrived she was going to look like something they found in a swamp along the way.

"But we couldn't have driven there, gotta take the long way in, through an entire forest," she grumbled.

"What?"

"Just said I'm glad it's a nice day."

Kara smiled at her and kept marching on. Lizzie huffed and puffed along behind her, cursing every tree root that she stumbled over. She could feel the energy draining out of her, like a leak in a pool. At this rate, she'd never make it back. She was sure she'd fall over dead if she tried. Her friend's excitement had given her the boost to make it this far, but she'd let them down soon enough.

Stupid broken body, stupid lazy legs. Why can't you be normal like everyone else? Why can't you be fun like Kara?

Lizzie's jealous self-loathing continued for the rest of the hike, only broken by Paul's announcement that they'd arrived at the gardens. The trio checked in with the Welcome Center to get their tickets and Lizzie watched as Kara grabbed one of every guidebook and map. She could barely hear her friends talking over the thrumming in her head as she trudged along behind them.

"Lizzie?" Kara spoke.

"Huh?"

"I was trying to figure out what section to start in. Did you want to cast a vote?"

"Umm, I don't know. Where are the rides?" Lizzie replied.

"What? What rides?"

"I don't want to walk anymore."

"Well, there's nothing here to trolly you around," Paul chimed in.

Kara looked her up and down, then frowned. "You should have said something. If you couldn't do this, you should have spoken up."

Lizzie sighed in defeat. "I tried, but you were so excited that I couldn't get it across."

"So, what do you want us to do?'

"Just go on as you planned. Let me find a place to sit and rest for a while, okay?"

Kara nodded and handed a map to Lizzie. Grabbing Paul's hand, they left to start their tour.

After buying a frozen lemonade from the snack cart, she moved to the furthest group of benches along the exit path. Lizzie knew she wouldn't catch up with her friends, so she might as well make it easy for them to find her.

Rehydrated and off her aching feet, she took her time reading over the guidebook Kara had given her. There were so many things to do, they could probably spend the entire day here. It was beautiful. What she could see around her looked like something out of a fairytale, stone pillars, and flowery shrubs, and they weren't even the real attractions.

Maybe I could go for a short walk, not far.

The nicely paved walkways should have been easier to navigate than the wooded path, but after a few minutes Lizzie's knees had given up, they popped and clicked. She found an empty picnic table set near a small greenhouse surrounded by ivy trellises. It was quiet in this little corner of the gardens. The greenhouse didn't appear to be open to the public, caution tape hung across the door.

As Lizzie sat recouping her energy, she watched the silhouette of a woman working in the closed greenhouse. She danced as she worked. Bouncing and twirling her way around the inside of the structure, a ballerina in baggy coveralls. Her curly locks bouncing as she picked up plants and moved them to another row.

Another carefree person enjoying life. Lizzie's gaze drifted out past the gardens, into nothing as she became lost in her thoughts.

"Flowers rarely make people sad."

The woman from the greenhouse stood in front of Lizzie, head tilted, looking at her. She laughed as Lizzie jumped in surprise, her freckled nose crinkling.

"You're sitting here frowning, looking a bit out of place among all the bright and lively greenery." She spoke with a subtle accent.

"I'm sorry. I was just—"

"I didn't say you had to apologize."

"Right, I was just thinking, I guess. Didn't realize I was making a face."

"Plenty of people come here to wander and think. You don't seem like it was your idea, though."

The woman moved to sit down next to Lizzie on the bench, settling a small crate in her lap.

Unloading her problems on a stranger wasn't exactly polite. Lizzie was tempted to make an excuse and move to another part of the park, but as the woman turned towards her and smiled, she felt like this was a rare opportunity. Someone who genuinely wanted to listen.

"I agreed to come with my best friend. She wanted to do the hike and tour of the gardens for her birthday. Now I've disappointed her because my body couldn't handle the hike and I've got no energy left for fun. I'm tired, everything hurts, and I don't know how to be like a normal person anymore. I hate being the sick one." Lizzie spoke in a rush, holding back tears.

The woman nodded, her copper-colored curls bobbing along.

"I understand exactly what you mean," she said. "I had terrible crippling pain in my back for years, could hardly stand for more than a few minutes without wanting to cry out. Couldn't get around without help. I always felt like an inconvenience to everyone else."

"I just watched you over there, dancing around."

"I know, isn't it great? Everything's so much better now."

"How?" Lizzie asked.

"I found this beauty."

Reaching into the wooden crate, she pulled out a newspaper-wrapped clod of dirt with a single deep green shoot inside.

"Meet Eve," she said.

Lizzie raised an eyebrow at it. Plants were not in her wheelhouse at all.

"It's… nice."

The woman laughed.

"I know it looks like nothing. This is just a baby, though. Freshly planted from my own little miracle plant."

"What do you do with it?"

"Care for it."

"So it's just like a regular houseplant. I'm terrible at those. Is this some kind of therapy exercise?"

"No, no, this is something special. This took away my pain. I found it when I was at my lowest, had to travel halfway across the world for it and it's finally given me seedlings. If you take care of the plant, it will take care of you. Here, take it. I promise, your life will *bloom*."

Lizzie took the plant. It was heavy for such a small thing, the newspaper slightly damp at the edges. She held it away from her, afraid it might dump soil in her lap. Grabbing her empty cup, she set the plant inside, settling it in gently.

"Ow—"

Lizzie pulled her hand back, a pinprick of blood welling to the surface on the side of her finger.

"Careful there, just a baby thorn, but now it knows you," the woman said with a smile. "Now you listen to me, you absolutely cannot let it wilt. If it does, you'll have no help, and good luck with your doctors. But when it's in bloom, I swear, you'll have

the peace you wish for so badly."

Lizzie nodded her head in understanding, even though she still wasn't sure whether she'd keep the thing alive. The woman smiled at her once more before waltzing away just as silently as she'd arrived. Glancing at her phone, Lizzie saw an hour had passed since they'd arrived. Kara and Paul were nowhere in sight, and she was feeling the effects of the park bench on her spine. Sending off an apology text to her friends, she arranged for a ride back to the apartment, knowing they'd be disappointed.

Clearing off her bedside table, Lizzie arranged the new pot she'd picked up that morning. It was a little large for the baby-sized plant, but she'd filled it out with fresh soil, hoping it would provide more room to grow than the lemonade cup. Three days had passed and a new leaf was already budding. The plant was thriving, her friendship wasn't.

They'd barely spoken to each other since the failed birthday hike. She was sure Kara was expecting some sort of apology, but she honestly didn't feel she should have to apologize for her health. In the past, she might have, profusely. *Maybe there's something to this plant thing, after all. Is standing my ground considered healing?*

Satisfied with her plant baby's new situation, Lizzie eased open the blinds to give them both a little sunlight before settling herself into bed with her trusty lap desk. If her boss knew she did most of her work this way, in yesterday's pajamas, they'd probably cringe.

It was easier for her. She had a routine. After an hour of sorting through emails, she'd get up, stretch, and refill her water bottle. Checking in with her plant she noticed it needed little water as well. *Alright then, a drink for me and a drink for you.* During lunch, they moved over to the windowsill to bask in the fresh air and warm sun. Normally, after she was done with her reports, she'd clean herself up and join Kara in the kitchen before dinner. They'd chat about the day and maybe share a drink. But that wasn't happening right now. Instead, Lizzie changed into a new pair of pajamas and turned on the TV. With no one else around, she shared her commentary with the plant at her bedside.

The new routine continued throughout the week. Lizzie watched with excitement as her plant grew a little more each day. It began branching out into tiny hanging vines. As it grew, it needed water almost as often as she did. If she was late in taking a break, its leaves would all fall to one side. As if fainting dramatically. It made her nervous.

She didn't want to fail. Kara had knocked at her door the night before, with an offer of pizza. Lizzie had made an excuse, not wanting to leave the plant alone. She didn't think Kara would appreciate her carrying it to dinner. Her friend had referred to it as "destined for the dumpster" when Lizzie had mentioned bringing it home. She felt bad lying about not feeling well. It was the exact opposite. She felt great. She'd been sleeping so much better, and her back hardly ached after all day hunched over her laptop.

Eve was her responsibility now. She might even say it was

11

her best friend. At least the plant would never look at her with pity or disappointment. So Lizzie ignored Kara's attempts at trying to get her out of her room, emerging to eat whenever her roommate was at work. When she had to leave the house, she made the trips as short as possible. The more she returned home to a drooping plant, the less she bothered with those trips. Trash and dirty clothes were piled up next to the bed. She was reluctant to leave the room long enough to do the laundry. Eve didn't care whether Lizzie wore yesterday's clothes. She grew greener regardless.

Kara and Paul had gone on a trip upstate for their anniversary. She'd knocked on Lizzie's door at least fifteen times yesterday before they left, wanting to be sure everything would be fine. They seemed to think she'd slipped into some sort of depressive episode, which was ridiculous. She'd never felt better.

A gust of wind blew the rain in through her window, sprinkling her and Eve with water. It felt nice, almost warm against her skin. Lizzie was lying in bed again. She'd used her extra energy to push it across the room, closer to the window she never closed anymore.

She'd perched her plant on a stand next to her. Its long, fern-like vines spread across her sheets. She'd woke up that morning to find her arm tangled in them. Wiggling it only made them wrap up tighter. Not wanting to jostle the plant too much, she relaxed and let it be.

"It's only the left one. I don't need it right now."

Turning on the TV, she rested, reaching over for the

occasional sip of water from the bottle next to the bed. The time ticked by and it never crossed her mind to move, her body didn't feel the need to.

Slowly, the vines crept further, snaking themselves around her shoulder and down across her ribs. Lizzie slept without a single restless twitch and woke to laze in the sun when it emerged. She smirked as she examined her precious plant with her free hand. It had grown so lovely and flower buds had finally popped up. Soon it would bloom. Soon she'd be healed. She believed it now, completely. The doubts had washed away with all her pain. Nothing hurt anymore.

"Good morning, Eve," Lizzie said, nuzzling a leaf with her cheek.

The plant had grown wild overnight, trailing its deep emerald leaves across her body. Its stone planter now sat on her sternum, a wide crack forming along the base where the roots had snaked out. She couldn't move anymore, not that she bothered to try. Instead, she admired the largest bud that had formed at the head of her plant. Its outer leaves were almost ready to part.

"What color will you be? Something bright and tropical, or something deep and romantic? I bet it'll be beautiful, and I'll have done it all by myself."

Lizzie grinned with pride, careful not to let her shallow breathing disturb the spreading roots.

"Lizzie, I'm home. Lizzie, why is it so warm in here? Lizzieee…"

Kara dropped her bags on the couch and made her way through the silent apartment. She knocked on the door to her friend's room and heard no answer. She'd hoped Lizzie would be in a better headspace when she returned. It worried her.

"Lizzie I—"

Kara stood slack-jawed, holding the door open. The room's furniture had all been turned around and the floor was littered with empty water bottles. The biggest shock sat against the far wall. Where it looked like Lizzie had planted a garden in the middle of her bed. Horror morphed into confused anger as she saw no sign of her so-called best friend.

"You've got to be kidding me. This is ridiculous!"

Paul followed her shouting across the living space and stared at the mess, equally perplexed.

"Where did that thing come from?"

"There's dirt everywhere," Kara shouted. "Is this the stupid plant she brought home from the park?"

"It looks exotic and kind of wild," Paul answered.

"Well, they can have it back then."

Kara looked up the number to the garden park and paced the hallway while trying to explain the situation. After a brief hold and a transfer, they finally put her through to someone who knew what she was talking about. The friendly voice told her to leave it be, and they'd send someone over right away to collect it.

To counteract her stress, Kara began scrubbing every surface of the kitchen. She expected Lizzie to walk through the door any minute and they'd have a fight over the state of her room. When

the knock on the door came, Paul ushered in a slight woman with a head full of curls. They showed her the room, and she squealed with excitement, bouncing around the bed on her tiptoes.

"Oh, hello there. My beauty. Look at you, so healthy. You've bloomed, truly, and I'm so happy for you. So well fed you are, and so many precious little seeds you'll be giving me." The woman turned to them, beaming, her eyes sparkling the same deep emerald as the plant she was admiring.

"I'm so glad you called. Lizzie will be such a wonderful addition to our nursery."

The Grace Fruit

Kristen Bazen

Tessa Northwood had already killed the dahlias. Her parsley plant still owned one pair of green leaves, but it too was on its deathbed. Soon, she would have to add the dried and wilted herb to her compost bin, the graveyard of all her plant projects since starting college. The bin was already full of succulents, which were supposed to be easy to care for.

When her mama came up the front porch steps carrying something green and leafy, Tessa's heart floundered. Her mama had green thumbs and green toes and believed everyone had the same knack for natural things as she did. Her vast garden sprouted and blossomed at all the right times, yielding crisp vegetables and exquisite flowers. Weeds hardly dared to show their faces and fled before her ready hoe and rake.

"I ran out of room in my garden, dear, so I brought you a tomato seedling." Mama extended the terra cotta pot, her eyes bright and cheery, though Tessa knew the pain of loss lurked beneath. It was a loss she felt herself, mingled with the heaviness of guilt.

Flicking a wave of blonde back over her shoulder, Tessa cautiously wrapped her hands around the pot, half-expecting the young plant to shrivel and die right before her eyes.

"Thanks, Mama. That's really sweet of you." Hopefully the thing lasted at least a week.

Mama dusted off her hands. "Anytime, my dear. Once it gets a little warmer, plant her in full sun, water early in the morning, and give her a little fertilizer rich in phosphorus. None of that high-nitrogen stuff. I have extra bean plants too, if you want them."

Mercy, no. "I think I'll stick to the tomato plant," Tessa said, adjusting her grip on the pot. "I have exams to study for." Never mind that it was the end of April and she only had another week of college classes.

"And you still have the parsley to take care of." Mama smiled and kissed Tessa's cheek.

Well, yes. One or two leaves, perhaps.

Long after Mama had gone home, Tessa stood on the porch of her little house, holding the tomato plant like a child she didn't know what to do with. In the end, she decided the back patio would be as good a spot to die as any, and she settled the pot on the low wall around the seating area.

"That's not going to work."

Tessa looked up at the flat prediction of doom. Her next-door neighbor, prickly Maureen Finley, was shaking her head, the afternoon sun making a nest of light in her curly gray hair.

The houses in their neighborhood were too close together, and the lack of fences was a severe oversight. Pressing her lips together, Tessa slid her hands into the pockets of her pale blue jeans in mild defiance.

"Why not?" Her words were more a challenge than a question.

"There's not enough sun there," Maureen said, pointing to the nearby maple tree. Her words were quick, choppy, and unsympathetic. "That part of your yard is shaded most of the day. Tomato plants need full sun."

Maureen delighted in pointing out faults and failures. Criticism and complaint seemed to be her daily bread, and Tessa couldn't remember a single positive interaction with her neighbor. Last fall, she had raked her leaves into Tessa's yard, and the year before that, she had picked the pretty tulips Tessa's mama had planted and put them in a vase in her own kitchen—plainly visible through the window facing Tessa's home.

Grace received becomes grace given, Mama always said. But Tessa was convinced that if she extended grace to her neighbor, the woman would chew it up and spit it back into her face.

"My tomatoes were prize-winning last year," Maureen continued. "The largest in the neighborhood. And my cucumbers, too."

Blah, blah, blah.

"I'm happy for you." The sarcasm bled through her threadbare politeness, and Tessa turned to go inside before she said anything else unkind. The tomato seedling remained in the shade.

On her way upstairs, she smoothed the lavender tablecloth in her dining room and adjusted the pale green vase filled with baby's breath—dead and dried, of course. In her bedroom, Tessa rearranged the paintbrushes on her desk, threw away a crumpled pencil drawing, and folded a rose-colored sweatshirt she had brought from the laundry room.

Only desaturated colors were allowed in her décor and closet. Pastels. Soft, gentle, calming tones. Anything but the bright red and blue of the police cars, the blinding lights that had blazed through her windshield one icy night last winter. Anything but the bold green and yellow of the ambulance that had taken away her brother.

Digging her nails into her palms to stop the memories, Tessa turned toward her easel and met her brother's smiling eyes, sketched in graphite. How he had looked before the accident, before her car spun on black ice and smashed the passenger side into a wide oak tree.

His name was Owen.

Her family reminded her often that his death hadn't been her fault, but Tessa still carried the staggering burden of guilt. It was the ice, they would say. There was nothing she could have done. And yet, she was sure if only she had been driving more slowly, been paying more attention, or reacted with less panic, the outcome would have been different.

Her mama's blonde hair wouldn't have turned white so soon. Her papa wouldn't walk with his back stooped and shoulders hunched. And her little brother would still be lighting up the

house with his laughter and eyes full of mischief.

Tessa picked up a charcoal pencil and began shading and smudging near the bridge of Owen's nose. Slowly, carefully, his features took shape under her hand. She had already sketched the contours with graphite, and now, her brother seemed to come alive again as she moved the charcoal back and forth, creating depth and highlights and the crinkles in his nose that showed when he smiled.

Strangely, as Owen's features became more life-like, Tessa's mind wandered back to the tomato plant on her back patio. How long until the leaves withered from lack of sun? How many days until the green, living matter decayed into dust and scattered to the wind? The images wouldn't go away, and she pressed the charcoal deep into the shadows of Owen's hair, resisting.

All her previous plant projects had been failures. What was the use of continuing to try coaxing life from a collection of leaves? Paints and pencils she could control. But plants had a mind of their own, and they came to her house to die.

Tessa picked up a kneaded eraser, intending to bring out the highlights in her brother's hair, but it was no use. She pretended not to care and told herself it didn't matter, but she was tired of death and decay. Of reminders that this world wasn't all what it should be.

The small, ordinary act of watering and weeding could be a way to give life. Had she ever put her heart and soul into the plant-gifts from her mama? Or had she given them mediocre care, afraid that if she put forth full effort, she would discover

her all wasn't enough?

Well, no longer. Her brother would never again walk this earth, but perhaps in caring for an infant plant, she could bare her teeth against the dark. Setting down her eraser, Tessa stomped outside. Nothing more would die on her watch—not even a stupid tomato plant.

The seedling was still intact for the hour it had spent in the shade, and she let out a soft breath of relief. Casting a furtive glance over her shoulder, she saw that Maureen was still tinkering in her yard, but was bent over some flowering shrub.

Quickly, quietly, Tessa wrapped her arms around the pot and tiptoed to her front yard, where she laid it to rest on a flat stone. Did it need water? Or maybe some fertilizer? What kind had her mama said again? Something with nitrogen, maybe? Yes, tomorrow she could run to Lowe's and pick up a small bag.

After a few more hours spent on Owen's portrait—her final project for drawing class, Tessa switched her lamps from 5000 Kelvin to 2700 Kelvin. All the lights in her home had to be exactly the same temperature. No mixing of yellow and white lights. The pure white for daytime, the warm tones for evening.

She locked her front door, checked it three times, and drew the curtains over the windows facing the street. All was as it should be, but Tessa was still anxious.

The morning wasn't much better. She woke up with a knot in her stomach. Heaving a deep sigh, she threw aside the covers. Why should something as insignificant as a tomato plant disrupt her equilibrium?

The seedling would be thirsty after its long night, so Tessa filled a glass with water and stepped outside on bare feet. The wood was cold and smooth under her toes, and the morning breeze promised a warm spring day. She tipped the cup and watched the dry earth soak up her offering. Maybe this time, her plant project would survive. Maybe this time, her hands could give life instead of squelching it.

"You're giving it too much water."

Tessa startled at Maureen's voice, and she turned, irritation prickling under her skin. There was her neighbor, pruning her perfect hedges.

"I like my vegetables well-hydrated," Tessa said, raising her chin.

Maureen scoffed. "Shows what you know. And tomatoes are a fruit, not a vegetable."

"If you like tomatoes in your fruit salad, that's fine by me." Tessa clenched her cup and escaped back into the house before Maureen could reply.

Her mama would say that *everyone has a story, and no heart is without a wound.* Tessa thought Maureen used her words like needles just for the fun of drawing blood.

For several weeks, the plant grew steadily, and new leaves unfurled to catch the sun rays. With the danger of frost being past, Tessa planted the seedling in a place of honor next to her porch steps. To create a space where the seedling would thrive, she used most of the decaying matter from her compost bin, which included the parsley that had at last given up the ghost. Every morning before going to work at the downtown bakery,

she watered her tomato plant, and when coming back home just before dinnertime, she checked to make sure the plant was still green and growing.

Tessa's charcoal drawing of Owen now hung above her bed, and she had passed her classes with excellence. The tomato plant grew and spread its sharp-lobed leaves, and she grew more confident. Maureen continued to shake her head at their morning water meetings, saying it was too tall, too leafy. Tessa only smiled quietly to herself, convinced her neighbor was just jealous. The tomato plants next door weren't flourishing nearly as well as hers.

Spring deepened into a warm Michigan summer, and one morning in mid-July, Tessa stepped outside with her waterpot. There was Maureen, not in her own front yard, but in Tessa's, and poking at her precious tomato plant.

Tessa stopped short, her ire rising. "What are you doing in my yard?" She demanded. Holding the waterpot like a weapon, she strode down the porch steps.

"Your plant has a disease," Maureen said, pointing to some small, wrinkly leaves. She sounded entirely too satisfied.

Narrowing her eyes at her nosy neighbor, Tessa stepped closer to look at the leaves in question. Was that a yellowish fringe overtaking the living green? "That's new growth," she said, willing the words to be true.

"No, those leaves are dying." Maureen straightened. "You must not have fertilized it. Tomatoes need soil rich in nutrients."

Dying.

 23 

Tessa's heart grew cold at the word. "I did give it fertilizer. The kind that's high in nitrogen."

"Nitrogen?" Maureen barked a laugh. "No wonder. Your plant put all its energy into leaves and left none for the fruit."

"Vegetable," Tessa muttered. So she had given it the wrong fertilizer. How had she managed to mix them up?

"My plants already have little green tomatoes," Maureen continued, nodding to herself. "Sure to be the biggest in the neighborhood."

"Then why are you poking around mine?" Tessa glared at her neighbor.

Maureen stiffened. "No need to get all huffy with me. I was just being neighborly." She stomped back to her yard, as if Tessa was the one in the wrong.

Conflict made her anxious, so Tessa stopped watering her plant before work. Instead, she went out around midnight with her waterpot, cloaked by the dark. She wouldn't run into Maureen then, and neither would she see the tomato plant dying.

But several nights later, even by moonlight, she could see the big leaves curling up, giving up. She was failing, again. Causing death, again. After retreating to her room, she sat with lights out and windows open, staring at the stars.

Why did everything have to die?

The air felt heavy with old wounds that had never quite healed. The warm night wind whispered through the trees, and crickets filled the air with song, oblivious to the weight of grief. Another question came.

Why did she get to live?

Maybe there was a different way to defeat the dark. A way besides keeping a tomato plant alive. Mama's voice echoed in her mind once more. *Grace given becomes grace received.*

Was there something deeper here? From her Creator, she had received breath, received love, received life…wasn't it all grace? And if life was grace received from God, maybe giving grace meant giving grace to others. Even to prickly neighbors.

Tessa's heart rebelled against the thought. Give grace to Maureen, who had been a thorn in her yard since the day she moved in? What would giving grace even look like? It would be harder than keeping a tomato plant alive.

No ideas presented themselves before sleep came, or the next day. Tessa stopped going out at midnight and didn't water the plant at all. What was the use? She would only be forced to watch green leaves shrivel and fade to brown matter that would crumble if she touched it. Maureen would come to gloat, and then Tessa would be the one shriveling. From her west window, she had a perfect view of Maureen's tomato plants, which were full of ripening fruit.

It was several weeks before she dared to glance again at the decaying plant next to her porch, but as she went out to get the mail one afternoon, she caught a flash of red through bits of green and brown. Her heart lurched. Had she given up too soon?

Gingerly, she reached out a hand and parted the leaves, some living, some dead, some fallen. There, nestled behind the

thick stem and other leaves still living, was the largest tomato she had ever seen.

In awe, Tessa stared at the round orb, hardly trusting her eyes. Despite her fumbling efforts, the seedling had indeed produced a tomato. And it was beautiful. Flawless. The sunlight caught the smooth, red skin, and it seemed to shimmer like a veiled jewel.

"My plants have a lot more tomatoes than that."

At the familiar voice from behind, Tessa pressed her lips together and turned, using all her available self-control not to snap a response.

Grace. That was what she had decided, right? But it was so hard. And her neighbor stood with a smug tilt to her chin, trowel still in hand.

Reigning in her pride, Tessa nodded. "You're right," she said. "I'm not much of a gardener. You seem to know a lot about growing plants."

Maureen blinked. Her thin lips opened and closed several times, and she cleared her throat. When she spoke, her voice was subdued. "Your tomato is bigger than all of mine, though."

Grace given, grace received. At her neighbor's surprising concession, Tessa felt more alive than she had since Owen's death. More words of grace came out before she could stop them.

"Do you want to come in? I have lemonade and cookies."

Silence met her offer. Maybe it was too much to expect after years of tension. Tessa fiddled with a bracelet on her wrist and awkwardly turned to go back inside.

As she reached the top step, her neighbor finally spoke.

"No one's ever invited me in before." A tremor made Maureen's voice wobble.

Tessa paused at the door and at last understood. Underneath the prickles were wounds.

"Well, I'm inviting you now," she said gently, and Maureen followed her inside, almost tiptoeing, as if the invitation might be retracted.

The cookies weren't homemade, and the lemonade was a little too tart, but the refreshments were a gentle demolition of barriers. Maureen asked about the photograph of Owen on her fridge, and Tessa learned that Maureen had lost her husband in a work accident. In the sharing of sorrows, Tessa found startling healing. In the giving of grace, somehow she had received it in return.

Magical
Green

Erstwhile

Kathryn Reilly

Masked, the seed waits

in darkness

for warmth and wet.

protected, it bides time

knowing the world

will align itself

eventually.

Inspired,

it cracks,

stretching limbs

trusting that something

lays

ahead

above

beyond

that will

relish

its worth.

Sweet Waking

Beka Gremikova

lora paused on the threshold of the Dream Mines and took a steadying breath. *All I need is a nightmare.* For the past century, she'd mined dreams to occupy herself while waiting for the chance to break her sleeping curse and escape the Dream Realm.

Tonight, that chance had arrived. Alora shook out her limbs, nerves buzzing. One hundred years to the day Nijak's curse had fallen, and now she would scare herself awake. If she didn't—she shuddered as the images crawled into her mind. She'd be nothing but a skeleton trapped in a castle swallowed by thorns. Such was her curse—wake up *exactly* one hundred years later, or die. Lord Nijak's curse was plain and simple— and disgustingly cruel.

Well, she *would* wake up. She *would* see her family again in the Open Eyes World and finally attend university to study dream cultivation. She'd fulfill her dreams and spite Lord Nijak, who'd cursed her when her family took King Ephrem's side in the bitter battle over the Dream Realm.

Squaring her shoulders, she stepped into the mine, snatching a pickaxe from the row of them leaning against the wall. Green veins streaked the pearly rock that arched around her. Some led to dreams, and others to the nightmares she sought. She swallowed. What little magic she possessed was only enough to mine one nightmare, and if she didn't choose the right one, it might destroy the entire Dream Mine.

Too bad Ephrem wasn't here to offer advice. On the occasions when he could visit, he'd always helped her find the best dreams to entertain herself. His knack for knowing what veins led to different dream types was astonishing. If anyone could help her find a terrifying nightmare, it was him. But she rarely saw him nowadays with the fighting so constant.

The only other way out of the Dream Realm for a mortal was True Love's Kiss. She grimaced. *And there's no way I want one of those right now.*

She was on her own.

She stepped closer to a dark vein in the rock, noting golden petals spattered through the green. She sighed. Probably another dream of frolicking through a wooded glade. She'd had enough of *those.*

Nearby, a lighter line of green streaked the wall, marbled with blood-red smears and dancing, sword-shaped slivers.

Far more nightmarish-looking. She hefted her pickaxe and chipped at the rock around the vein. The magic within her stirred, leaping from her body in a blaze of sparks to spatter across the shimmering stone.

Hissing filled the cavern. A hulking, furry *marikit* appeared, its fangs glistening, bulbous eyes locked on her face. It licked its lips, a growl rumbling from its throat.

The cavern trembled, rock grating in her ears. Her pulse raced. If she remembered her few dream cultivation studies properly, that was her consciousness shifting. Now, the *marikit* just had to attack her fully, and the adrenaline should shock her awake...Someone barrelled past her, blocking her way. She blinked in astonishment at a prince dressed head to toe in green, waving a sword like it was no heavier than a stick.

"Fear not, lovely princess!" He shouted.

Oh, no. *He* was part of the nightmare? Or was this even a nightmare? What if she'd run into someone's heroic fantasy?

The prince parried, and the marikit skittered backward, light on its feet for such a large monster.

"No! I need that nightmare!" Alora latched onto the prince's arm. The cavern trembled under their feet, and both Alora and the prince staggered forward. The *marikit* grunted, nearly losing its footing.

Alora caught herself before she fell. *That* was a stronger rumble than before. She glanced up, hopeful, but the quaking had ceased. Her fingers prickled with an odd sensation where they'd touched the prince's bare arm.

Maybe simply interacting with this nightmarish magical prince would be enough to rouse her consciousness?

The *marikit* howled and lunged. The prince shoved her aside, and she fell, smearing her gown with green-speckled dirt.

He hacked at the marikit, who swiped back at him with long, dark claws.

Alora jumped up, reaching out to grab his arm again.

The next instant, the prince struck the *marikit* between its ribs. The nightmare disintegrated, and the prince beamed at her before crumbling into fine green dust.

She stood there, arm still outstretched.

That was it. Her one chance, gone. She covered her face with a trembling hand and sank to the ground. The store of magic in her body had depleted; it'd take too long to recover itself enough for her to delve into another dream before the spell ran its course.

She'd never go to university. Never see her parents again. Her stomach twisted. She'd never speak with Ephrem again, either… Tears streaked down her cheeks.

Footsteps echoed along the tunnel, and she glanced up as a tall, rainbow-robed figure strode toward her. Her heart leapt. She quickly wiped the tears from her face and sucked in a deep breath. She didn't want the Dream King to catch her crying.

Ephrem's long, dark-green hair billowed like a sail in his wake. "Alora! I'm glad to see you—and my mines—are still in one piece!" He stopped beside her, shaking his head at the pile of green dust at their feet.

"Not for long if I don't wake up," she snapped, dragging her sleeve across her nose before staggering upright. "I thought you were too wrapped up with Nijak to help!"

"There's been a break in the fighting. Even Nijak's troops get tired." Ephrem cracked his knuckles. "But I'm here now, and

we're going to wake you up. Without breaking anything."

"Or kissing," she said, crossing her arms. "We don't know each other *that* well for a True Love's Kiss to work." *Yet.* Maybe one day. When she had the time to sort out her feelings in the Open Eyes World and it could be her choice—not because breaking a curse required it. She rubbed her fingers together, considering how the tunnels had trembled when she touched the prince's arm. "Do you know anything about magic being affected by touch other than True Love's Kiss?"

He shook his head. "Not that *I've* heard of, but…" He grinned sheepishly. "You're also the first sleep-cursed princess that I've ever met. You want me to try something else?"

She nodded.

His brow furrowed. "If it doesn't work—?"

"Try it first."

"All right." He faded from view as he crossed into the Open Eyes World. Alora held her breath.

Moments later, the cavern quivered. The glittering veins of green around her exploded into a dizzying blur… And she sat up in bed, blinking out at her own cozy chamber. Light green curtains fluttered in a soft spring breeze. Beside her, Ephrem held her hand. Magic tingled where his fingers clasped hers, the touch enough to trick the spell into releasing her from its grasp.

"It worked," Ephrem said, his eyes wide. "Imagine that. I never knew magic could be so gullible. Don't know why I didn't think of it sooner, really." He released her hand. "Far less painful than scaring yourself awake."

34

Alora stared down at her fingers, which still sparked with the lingering effects of magic. "What a fantastic area of dream study," she murmured. Nonconventional methods of lifting sleeping curses. Her fingers suddenly itched. "I need a quill and paper!"

Grinning, Ephrem found them at her nearby desk and carried them over. "Sweet Waking, Alora," he said as he handed her the quill.

Cursed

Cortney Manning

Thump. Thump. Thump. Someone was pounding on the front door. Beast rose, shaking off the cold that the drafty manor settled on even his fur-covered form. Foreboding tightened his limbs as he loped down his home's empty halls. Few dared enter his cursed land. Several years had passed since he'd seen another human—years in fact since he was human.

Pausing a moment to ensure his hood shaded the worst of his grizzled face, Beast balanced himself and drew open the door.

His heart thudded at the sight of a woman on his landing. For several moments, his mind insisted the Enchantress had returned, her form tall, slim, and graceful, perfectly proportioned in flowing trousers and an embroidered jacket. But this woman's head was swathed in gauzy green veils. The color was vivid, far more vibrant and warm than the grays and browns filling the prison in which Beast lived trapped.

Beast forced his breath to even out. The Enchantress's disguise had been the form of an old peasant, and, unlike this veiled woman, she did not cover her face and radiant beauty as she flung her curse against him.

Beast tugged at his own hood, shading his monstrous face. "Who are you? Why have you entered my estate?"

"My name is Helen." The woman spoke clearly despite the layers of gauze and silk. "I've traveled far in search of answers."

Her words were as cryptic as any enchantress. Beast frowned, feeling the fur rise on his arms. "I'm sorry, Miss. I doubt you'll discover answers here."

She stepped nearer. "Are you not the Beast?"

He tightened his grip on the door, carving its surface with his claws. "So, you heard about the Beast and traveled here to *gawk* at him?"

"*No.*" She shook her head with what seemed to be an earnest air. "My journey began long before I learned of your existence."

"Then why are you here?"

"I seek answers to break a curse."

Beast swallowed, his mind flashing to that stormy night when the hag he turned away became the Enchantress who ended his life. After bending his bones and reforging his flesh, she'd leaned down, whispering the cure to the destruction she'd wrought:

"*When you learn to love another, and she loves you in return, then you'll be restored.*"

She'd spoken as if offering a gift, yet what maiden could love Beast's hideous form?

He blinked at the woman standing at his threshold. Could

she be the key to his restoration?

"You've come to break my curse? Do you typically travel far and wide seeking such danger?"

Her green veiled face shook in the negative. "I travel because I enjoy it, or I did before…"

Beast narrowed his eyes. "Before what?"

Her shoulders dropped as she heaved a sigh. "As much as I'd love to break your curse, it's *my own* that I hope to end."

Beast unconsciously leaned nearer, trying to glimpse the face she hid beneath her veil. "You've been cursed, too?"

She fingered the edge of her outer veil. "I'll show you if you allow me three things."

Curious, Beast agreed. "Name them."

"Show me your face first."

A gasp sounded in his throat like a growl. No one had seen his face since the night of the curse.

"What else?"

"Grant me shelter in your home."

Her words, so similar to the Enchantress's, dug into the painful recesses of his regret. "Why?"

"For my third condition: work with me to find a way to end *both* our curses."

She stepped nearer, so close, he thought he saw her eyes flash beneath her gauzy veils. "Do you agree to these terms?"

Beast swallowed. If he removed his hood, she might run from him, like everyone else in his life but, if he refused, he'd certainly remain alone.

"I do." Before he could change his mind, Beast flung his hood back, allowing sunlight to touch his marred features.

Though he couldn't see Helen's face, she didn't draw back. Beneath her shield of veils, he sensed her direct gaze on him. Then she lifted her hands and began unwinding the verdant fabric from her face. Her fingers moved gracefully as Beast wondered what horrors she hid beneath her fabric armor. He realized he was holding his breath, dreading this being who didn't flinch at his hideousness. Slowly, he forced himself to exhale. What kind of monster would he be if he shrank back from another cursed face?

Her outer veils were gone now, piled on the flagstones at their feet. Then she removed the final gauzy fabric.

Anger pounded through Beast's veins at the features she revealed, and he yanked his hood back over his head. "*You lied!*"

Helen gestured to her flawless skin, ruby lips, and limpid eyes. "I am cursed."

Beast reached for the door, intending to shut out the imposter, but she pushed her shoulder into the doorway so he could not close it without crushing her.

"Not all curses are the same." She crossed her arms. "Tell me, what's your name?"

"Surely you know," he spat. "I'm the Beast."

"Exactly. Though you had a name before the curse, you've lost it beneath your appearance. I told you my name is Helen, but without my veils, I'm denied my name, too. The people call me Beauty."

"Even if it's true, beauty is no curse."

Her face tightened grimly. "When your face causes conflict wherever you go, it's a curse. When kings and warriors fight for your hand no matter the cost, it's a curse. When you're valued only for your looks and told to silently accept your luck no matter how it hurts you or your homeland, it's a curse. Not all curses look the same, but that doesn't mean they pain you any less."

Beast eased his grip on the door. "So... you didn't lie. You truly wish to help?"

"Yes."

Beast slowly drew open the door and tried not to stare at Helen's beautiful features.

Before he knew what she intended, her hand gripped his claw in an earnest handshake.

"Thank you—what is your true name?"

"Andrei." The word felt foreign in his mouth.

"Thank you, Andrei." Her brilliant smile lit the hallway more vividly than the green of her veils, but it was the sound of his name on another's lips that truly warmed Andrei's soul at last.

SORROWFUL
GREEN

Someday

Anne J. Hill

This is where things
   Come to be buried,
   To die and rest
Beneath the soil

Upheaving dirt
One shovel-full at a time
Until metal hits bone
With a shattering crack

This is where
The buried lay
Beneath the earth
In the darkness

I lay me down to sleep
Beneath the soil
Amongst the bones
My time has come

This is where
The living bury
The dead and gone
Beneath the old oak tree

Its leaves spring forth
Bringing new life
To where the bodies
Lay at last

This is where
We visit our loves
The ones who've gone away
Beneath the fertile soil

And this is where
With closed eyes
Thanking God above
They'll see me again
Someday

Wish Away

Julia Skinner

Bren, the sole second-born of the Liber tribe, ducked under a low branch before remembering that the action was unnecessary. *Ghosts don't have to worry about walking into things.*

And he was something *worse* than a ghost.

He wasn't anything at all.

As Bren continued forward, he glanced down at the thin vine wrapped around his left wrist. A single teardrop leaf stuck out from it, sickly faded green against his light skin. It was his *Wish*. The one he'd made three days ago, when he'd asked an ancient myth-book to wipe him from existence.

Towering gigan trees loomed all around him, stretching out their pale, sunlight-deprived limbs across the top of the jungle. The trees' huge, dark green leaves blocked out any trace of the sky above, hiding the tribes from the monsters who lurked beyond the jungle. On some of the thicker branches, there were a few houses, built high above the ground. Houses full of happy families.

You are a mistake. Black words crawled through his thoughts, voiced by everyone he'd ever met. *You shouldn't even be alive.*

Bren's stomach twisted, and he focused on the roots wound across the ground as they phased right through his feet. He'd been treated like a curse his entire life just because he was a second-born, but no one seemed to even remember *why.*

The only reason he'd survived infanthood was because his mother had, for some reason, decided to not abandon him to die in the wilderness like the tribe did to any of their accidental, extra children. Later, though, she decided she'd made a mistake, and moved to another tribe, leaving him and his brother behind.

That's all he was: a *mistake* to be abandoned, and forgotten.

So three days ago, curled up in the corner of his room after finding the myth-book in an old chest, he'd decided to make life better for everyone. *"I wish to stop existing,"* he'd whispered into its forbidden pages.

And now here he was: racing against time to reverse it.

Drek is probably happy to be rid of me. The words were jagged and dark, slicing straight to his heart. His older brother had grown up as an outcast because of him. What would he say when Bren showed back up?

Would he abandon him too?

A trail of cold bit into the skin around his wrist, and Bren let out a startled yelp. An ugly, rotting black slowly crept along the vine, covering the green. He froze for a moment, panic tightening around his throat like a snake as he watched the tiny leaf shudder.

Please don't fall. Please don't fall. Please don't fall.

 45 

Once it fell, that'd be… that'd be it. The book claimed that after making a Wish, you had three leaves, three days, before it became official, before he was just… *gone.*

No longer lingering in this in-between state.

Just gone.

I have to find the Mythrite, Bren clenched his jaw, stumbling forward again. He had lied. He didn't want to stop existing. He wanted to live—to be seen—so badly, his very bones ached. *She'll be able to fix me.*

Drek never thought he'd be traipsing around the jungle looking for a flower the size of his fingernail. It was dumb! It was humiliating! It was… *way* harder than it should be. He scowled at the ground as he stalked over the tangled roots.

The viri flower grows in the east section of the jungle, beyond the tribe's hunting grounds, the Mythrite had told him. *Green petals. White center. Cut the flower head off, leave the rest unharmed.*

He'd never even heard of the stupid viri flower until the other day when the Mythrite agreed to find his little brother in exchange for the rare petals. Three days ago he'd come home to find the house empty, the only trace of his brother was a wrinkled myth-book in the bedroom they shared. Nothing else. No other clues. And no one in the tribe would help.

"Good riddance!" They said. *"Count this as a blessing."*

But Drek *couldn't* just let him go!

Bren was his little brother! He was responsible for Bren!

And… he loved him. Drek had never admitted that before. Maybe he hadn't realized it before his brother disappeared. But now the world felt as though a piece had been ripped out of it, as if the colors in the jungle had faded to gray.

Drek's eyes started to burn, and he blinked, trying to focus on scanning the ground for the plant. *There's so many green things in the jungle!* How was he supposed to find a flower he'd never seen before?

But he *would*, even if it took him the rest of his life. He'd find the stupid flower, and he'd get his brother *back*.

The vine had turned completely black by the time Bren burst out into a small clearing with a hut at its center. The hut was strung together by a chaotic jumble of wood and vines, and it was on the ground. How had it not been overwhelmed by the ever-growing jungle? He shook his head, and crept forward, memories seeping into his mind.

He remembered peeking at this place from the trees when he was younger, him and his brother daring each other to go speak to the Mythrite.

"Bet she doesn't fear the monsters outside the jungle!" Drek has said. *"And she's probably killed loads of people!"*

The thought had freaked both of them out so much, they'd run all the way back home.

Swallowing hard, Bren stepped through the veil of leaves that made up the door, passing through as if they were made of

nothing more than air.

Inside, the hut had a hard-packed dirt floor, with a bed mat to the right, and a table and cooking area on the left. A woman hovered over a small fireplace, where a kettle hung, boiling.

The Mythrite.

Bren froze. He'd seen her before, of course. But… never *this* close. She looked a lot younger than she should have, seeing she'd been around for a really long time. The robe she wore looked like it had been pieced together by thousands of small black leaves. Bren squinted. Were those vines woven into her dark hair?

The Mythrite hummed as she placed three delicate teacups on the table, beside a dark, wrinkled book. His breath caught. *My myth-book! How did it get here?*

"Mythrite?" Bren said. She kept humming, rearranging the cups. Fear pricked down his spine, burning an icy chill into his veins. "Mythrite?" he repeated, louder. He reached for her arm, but his hand phased straight through her.

"Please see me," his voice cracked. "I didn't mean it, I didn't…" The Mythrite turned away, toward the kettle.

You were born a mistake, his mind hissed, *and you will die one as well.*

Black blinked across his vision as the voices of everyone in his past rose like a fog. Voices blaming him for every bad thing that happened in the tribe. Voices saying he shouldn't exist. Telling him about all the lives he'd made worse because he was alive.

You were never supposed to exist.

Everyone will be happier without you.

Your mum left because of you.

You are a curse.

He could *feel* their words, like mold, slinking across his soul, dragging him down into their depths. They pounded in his mind, over and over and over. A hateful drum that couldn't be silenced or dulled.

Mistake. Mistake. Mistake.

Bren sank to the ground. On his wrist, the edges of the leaf sharpened, crystalizing into cold, dark rock.

Today he was going to vanish forever.

And no one cares.

No one has ever cared.

Someone erupted through the hut's doorway, and Bren jerked his head up. A familiar, broad-shouldered young man stalked across the room, mud squelching off his body in globs. Disbelief thudded in Bren's chest. *It can't be…*

"You didn't tell me there was a mire in that part of the jungle!" The man spat.

Drek.

His brother was here? *How… why?*

"Yes, well," the Mythrite said airily, "that's the only place the viri flower grows. A small price to pay for my help, I would think."

Drek curled his lip in disgust, and tossed a small bag onto the table. "*There*. Now, where is my brother?"

The world seemed to freeze around Bren. He stared, open-mouthed, at his brother. *Drek's looking for me?*

He came to the Mythrite… to find me?

The realization was like a little sprout of life deep inside the black that had overtaken his mind.

"Ah," the woman checked her kettle. "Well, as you can see from the cups, I was expecting one other, but I haven't eyes of my own so that someone best speak up!"

"What does *that* mean?" Drek spat.

"It means," the Mythrite said, "I'm not the one who gets to decide whether your brother is brought back."

The hardened leaf on Bren's wrist vibrated weakly, as if gasping its last breath.

Drek stomped across the room, and slammed a hand on top of the myth-book. "Mythrite, you *will* find my brother for me, and you will do it right *now*."

He cares.

The words overlapped the others, green against black, consuming the darkness like the vines covering the hut.

Drek cares about me.

The Mythrite swept her gaze across the room, and he noted with a jolt that her eyes were filmed over by a white haze. "Do you know why second-borns are seen as curses?"

"No?" Drek scowled. "What does this have to do with—"

She held up a hand, "long ago, Mythrites were plentiful among the tribes. They were revered, respected, *wanted*. We wielded the magic in this jungle to help it grow, to both protect and heal it. The best of us could even alter reality. Until one day, a Mythrite did a terrible thing. From then on, the tribes worked to rid themselves of us, and so they began to reject their second-

borns." She turned to face Drek. "I am a Mythrite, yes, but a Mythrite is not made up of only one person. To weave magic, there must be two—a pair." She paused. "I... am alone, now. And I cannot bring your brother back on my own."

The tribes worked to rid themselves of us.

Bren pushed himself to his feet, a realization forming in his mind. *Does that mean...* he looked at Drek's hand on the myth-book. Slowly, he reached out, and placed his on top, pausing right before it sank through. He could feel *something*, thrumming in the air around them, just out of reach.

"What is it you wish for?" The Mythrite said. Somehow, Bren knew the question wasn't directed toward his brother. He squeezed his eyes closed.

You are a mistake.

They don't want you.

But someone *did*. And that was all that mattered.

"I wish to be seen," Bren whispered. *To be heard, to exist.*

Green erupted behind his eyelids. Slithering over every shadow, tangling around every jagged word that had ever been spoken to him. He gasped, stumbling back. It felt like, like *healing*, like finally getting a gulp of air after almost drowning, like cool rain on his skin after a blistering heatwave.

He opened his eyes and found the Mythrite standing in front of him. The delicate, hard leaf had fallen from the vine, and she'd caught it on the flat of her finger.

"*There you are*," she smiled.

Bren stood in frozen suspension. He couldn't move, afraid that

it wasn't real, that at any moment, he'd puff away into nothing.

The Mythrite blew on the leaf, and it evaporated. Then, leaning forward, she tapped the vine on his wrist. It was green again, somehow, and it wiggled as it unwound itself. The vine slipped onto the Mythrite's hand, moving up her arm like a tiny, featureless snake. "You aren't needed anymore, my dear Wish." She whispered to it.

"Am I back?" Bren said, "can you see me?"

"Obviously I can't," she said, "I'm *blind*."

"But how—"

"A Mythrite always knows her wishes." She waved a dismissive hand and stalked back to the boiling kettle.

"*Bren?*"

Bren looked up. His brother was staring at him, a mixture of shock and joy warring over his expression. Tears slipped down Drek's cheeks, forming pale streaks through the splotches of mud. The sight warmed the last of the ice encasing Bren's heart. He had *never* seen Drek cry, not even when their mother left them.

"Is it really you?"

Bren nodded, throat too tight to speak.

His brother grabbed his shoulders, as if to prove that he was there. "What did you do, Bren? Where... how..."

"I'm..." Bren glanced down, his voice barely audible. "I'm the mistake who ruined your life."

Drek paused, then enveloped him in a crushing hug. "You," he growled, "are not a mistake."

Something tore free inside him, like a wall of vines falling away, and the tears burning in his eyes slipped down his face, warm, and—*and real*. He was actually back. He was solid. Visible. *Alive*.

After a few moments, Drek pulled away. "But I don't understand, how did you just appear?"

Swiping the tears from his eyes, Bren picked up the myth-book, and turned toward the Mythrite. She was pouring tea into the three cups. "Mythrite?"

"Yes, yes," she set her kettle down, "I'll train you two."

"Train us…" Drek started.

"To be *Mythrites*," Bren whispered.

"Exactly." the woman said.

Warmth filled Bren's veins, the kind that coated the jungle's plants, causing them to grow, and grow, and grow.

I'm not *a mistake*.

The words were glowing, life-giving viridescent.

I'm a Mythrite.

The Last
Green Dragon

Hannah Carter

Nobody believed in the last green dragon anymore.

Biting wind pierced through Nadia's threadbare yellow scarf.

She tried to pull it up over her nose, to keep the shards of ice from scratching her delicate skin, but to no avail. It refused to stay up. Despite her mittens that Mama had sewed with extra love—her special brand of magic—Nadia's fingers felt numb and frostbitten.

It seemed like Mama's magic was fading, just like the rest of the country.

Zeleniva had once been a glittering world, full of night circuses, dancing bears, fantastical ballets, and magic. But then the ice dragons had swooped in and murdered the royal family and their allies, the green dragons. Any chances of thawing, spring or summer, had died in the White Revolution. Now, the bitter chill kept everyone inside, and the circuses and ballets had vanished. All of Zeleniva seemed dull and lifeless now, barren of the magic that had once inspired these fantastical wonders.

Nadia might have cried, but her tears would have become icicles on her pale cheeks.

But, there had been *rumors*. Rumors that Princess Lysithea had hidden the last green dragon before her execution. Some people even said that she lived, even now, spared from the fate of her family by resurrection magic.

For years, people had whispered that she guarded it, waiting for the right person to bring back verdant springtime and end the ice dragons' control—even now, so long after the Revolution.

Nadia shivered again. Regardless of whether or not anyone else believed the rumors, she did. And she hoped, more than anything, that a mousy twelve-year-old girl might be the right person to melt the icy heart of Zeleniva. After all, that was her magical gift—the ability to infuse hope. It was the word 'hope' that Mama had stitched onto Nadia's baby blanket and every article of clothing for twelve years. For Mama had hoped for a baby for so long. Years and years and years, and then…a baby whose name meant hope came bursting into the world, dark black hair, coal-black eyes. One who seemed to show her whole family that life still had meaning, even in the depths of the White Revolution's darkness.

The snow piled up to her soaked pant legs and stockings as she reached one of the plateaus on Ledyora. The Ice Palace, as it was called, loomed in front of her. In reality, though, it was nothing but a large cave, surrounded by a forest of icicles that were as thick as tree trunks. Others hung upside down, creating

the illusion of prison bars. It was quite fitting.

Nadia blew on her mittens and hoped her magic wouldn't fail her now.

She slipped in through the icy bars, praying what she was about to do wasn't as foolish as everyone believed it was. "Master Belkon! I call upon you as the leader of the white dragons!"

A gale pounded back against her, and she pulled her scarf around her.

Perhaps anyone else would have given up, but Nadia's magic burned bright inside her chest, as warm as the springtime the green dragon would bring.

The winter chill filled the cavern and rattled it under her feet. Nadia gasped as it settled deep within her bones, threatening to turn them brittle and snap them. Her body trembled as snow crept in some unseen crevasse and swirled around her. The flakes began to twist and twirl, forming something white and intangible. Nadia squinted—she could make out one head… two…no, three—a three-headed dragon.

Nadia shook, but only from the cold. She met his icy blue gaze with a powerful stare. "Master Belkon, I know who you are."

The dragon chuckled, which turned the floor to ice. Nadia slid but regained her balance before she could fall, though she had to shake out her boots before the glacial magic crept onto her.

"Everyone knows who I am." Belkon stalked forward, all three heads pointed at her. Nadia held her ground all the while. "I am winter itself, the ruler of all Zeleniva."

She shook her head. "No. I know who you really are—

56

or who you once were." She reached inside her light coat and grasped the necklace inside. She imagined the portrait inside, of her beautiful Mama, her wonderful Papa, and baby Nik. "You were once the human called Malonik."

Shards of ice exploded from Belkon's body. Nadia covered her face with her arms, but the particles still stung her cheeks and embedded themselves into her mittens.

This time, when the dragon spoke, the cavern rumbled with the timbre of his voice. "Never say that name again!"

"Malonik. The man of secrets; the queen's right-hand man. You were so strange, so unusual, that the citizens of Zeleniva thought you must have ensorcelled the queen to get a court position." Nadia's teeth chattered. "But they were wrong."

Belkon roared. A blizzard rocketed from his mouth, and the force of it knocked Nadia off her feet. She smacked against the cavern wall and her breath exploded from her chilled lungs. Pain rushed in to take its place, and the world seemed to spin— or perhaps the wind was so rough the snow fell at a slant?

"They knew nothing!" Belkon stalked forward. In this form, he could not hurt her, and he possessed no flame like the red dragons of old. He may have been immortal, but without clothing himself in flesh, he could only use the weather against her. "The queen was an ignorant fool!"

Chilled tears slipped down Nadia's cheeks. She fought for every spasmodic breath. She just needed enough air to finish the conversation. "And she betrayed you."

Belkon swiped a claw at her but didn't make contact. "What

do you know about her betrayal?"

"Everything." Nadia's grip tightened on her locket. She could feel the faint heat of Mama's love as it radiated off the jewelry. "I know that you can only take human form so long as you love a human. And you loved a human, very deeply. The queen's lady-in-waiting, Alyona."

"Her name is not fit to pass your lips." Belkon's ice crept closer to Nadia's boots. She should have scrambled away from it, but the blow she'd taken still hurt. She could feel the tips of her boots start to frost over. "How do you know this story? You are not old enough to have been alive back then."

Nadia bit back a smile as the thought of Mama and Papa's fireside stories filled her with joy—but more importantly, it stirred her magic: hope. "Your exploits are well-known, even now. Your myth has only grown as this dreadful winter lingers."

Malonik growled.

Nadia continued her story. "You and Alyona married and had a son, very early in your service to the royal family as chief advisor. He was a dragon-blood, a human born with strong weather magic in his veins. A boy who could command ice and fly…a very remarkable child."

Belkon's body flickered as the snow began to slow. "Your rumors could not know that. We kept Dominik's existence a secret."

"You did, but many things have come to light since then. Like how Lysithea fell in love with Dominik. But the queen disapproved. She did not want dragon blood to taint her bloodline. She tried to break them apart, but their bond only

grew stronger." Nadia could see her breath with every word she uttered. Outside, the roar of the never-ending winter pounded against the Ice Palace. "Princess Lysithea was quite the headstrong girl, so the queen sent her green dragons to attack. Her magic was dragon compulsion, a rare and dangerous magic, to make dragons bend to one's will. I'm sure it scared you, for yourself and your son. One person should not have the ability to take away another sentient being's free will."

Belkon's heads glanced at one another. One flashed its teeth, the other one licked its lips, and the third—the middle one—leaned in closer. "Tell me what you know of that dark day, pathetic human."

"I know that the queen compelled green dragons to kill Dominik. But Alyona was with Dominik and Lysithea that day, and when the dragons attacked, they murdered your wife, who was defending your son."

Belkon exhaled. A puff of frigid winter air washed over Nadia. "No. It killed both of them."

A burst of hope threatened to leap from Nadia's heart. She longed to share it with this grumpy old dragon, all three heads. "No! Don't you see—Lysithea and Dominik were too clever for that. They knew that the queen would try another attack on Dominik's life, so they faked his death. He hid behind her walls, in the secret tunnels, but there was no time to tell you before you declared war—the White Revolution. The royal family died, along with all of their green dragons. Everyone you held responsible for your family's deaths."

"And they will never rise from the ashes again."

"Except." The world seemed to hang in the balance. The wind died down outside, and all three heads leaned closer, their blue eyes meeting Nadia's own black ones. And the hope inside of her began to melt a little bit of the ice around her. "Except one of them didn't die."

"Impossible!" Belkon whispered. "I killed them all myself. My fellow white dragons and I made short work of them all before the queen could stop us."

"But you forgot the royal family's magic. Some might be more outwardly powerful, but one princess had the most powerful yet quiet magic of all." Nadia braced herself against the wall so she could pull herself upward. "Lysithea's love for Dominik, for Zeleniva, and her family would not let her die. If she perished there, Dominik would starve in the walls. The love that kept the last green dragon egg alive would cease. Her country would never see spring again, and her family would die out. Through her love, she lived."

"Then Lysithea will die!" The Ice Palace shook with Belkon's declaration. "I will hunt her down and kill her—"

Nadia reached out a hand. Her mittens passed through the middle dragon's head instead of stroking it. "Would you kill her daughter, too? Your granddaughter?"

Belkon's threats and curses broke. "My—*what*?"

"Lysithea and Dominik. They got away. The beloved princess and the dragon-blood. Although their families were destroyed by hatred and their country in ruins, they held fast

to love. And Lysithea knew that one day, she could reclaim the green dragon egg. The one you took from her nearly-dead hands, but the one she dearly hoped and prayed would be safe because of her love for it. That, just once, love would overcome hatred." Nadia cupped both hands under the dragon's chin, though she could not physically hold him. "And her love gave birth to me, Grandfather. A girl with hope in her veins, born on the darkest, snowiest of nights. A girl to be a bridge between the two families."

The snow began to shimmer and swirl. The form of a dragon loosened and dissolved, like the morning frost when the first rays of sun stroke its delicate form. Slowly, it rebuilt itself and assumed the form of a man as pale as the ice itself, dressed in matching clothes. The only thing that seemed to hold color were his magnificent eyes, blue as crystals.

Belkon—Malonik—seized her cheeks with trembling hands. Nadia undid her locket, to show her grandfather the family that had persisted with love despite such hatred.

"Oh." Malonik let out a strangled cry as he saw his son's face: older than he last saw it, though Nadia wondered just how much it had changed. "Dominik."

"Yes. Papa." Nadia met the gaze of her grandfather. "He says I have his mother's eyes."

Malonik brushed his chilled fingers across her cheekbones.

"Return the egg, Grandfather. End this winter before your bitterness costs more people their lives." Nadia sniffled. "Please. Let spring return. Let yourself return to us."

"But Alyona…" Malonik began.

"Grandmother would want her family to be together. She would want the flowers to come back." Nadia slowly wrapped him in a hug. His form was unfamiliar to her and gelid, but it still felt...natural. "Papa says she always loved flowers."

And with that soft whisper, the great Master Belkon, the magnificent Malonik, began to weep. Grandfather and granddaughter clung to each other, their tears intermingling until Malonik pulled away slowly. From within his deep sleeves, he brought forth a jade egg, the size of Nadia's head.

"I could never destroy it. Your mother's love magic is powerful indeed." He gently placed its weight into Nadia's arms. "So instead, I kept it with me, in the cold, so that it could never grow warm enough to hatch. If it is truly your desire, though...I hope your heart is warm enough to hatch this egg and bring back spring."

Nadia smiled. "No, Grandfather." She grasped his hand and placed it against the shell. She could already feel the egg quickening, ready to hatch after so many years of being denied the love and warmth needed to bring forth new life. "I hope—I know—you and I can bring back spring... together."

Sunken Treasure

Willow Whitehead

She slowly sinks to the bottom of the river
    Warm water easing both her body and her soul
    The world seems deeper,
more meaningful underwater

Water muffling the noise from the world above
Sunlight diffuses at the surface of the water
The algae casts a colored glow on the riverbed
Tinting the underwater world

If only she could abide here
If she had only been born a Naiad
Then she could stay in the water,
and study its inhabitants forever

As the air fades from her lungs,
she knows she must return to the surface

The Willow Tree Swing

Someday she would stay
Someday she would decide not to surface

To simply remain in the water
For eternity
And hope that it would be kinder to her
than the world ever was

Author Bios

In Story Order

Xanna Renae

Xanna Renae loves daydreaming about how to save her characters from the messes she puts them in. She can be easily found where tea is brewing and pages are turning in tandem with her purring cat.

She's currently giving life to the ideas in her head and has published a collection of fantastical short stories and poems *Through the Violet Redwoods*.

She is currently finishing her BA in Creative Writing from Southern New Hampshire University, where she is graduating Summa Cum Laude. You can find her online talking about writing, publishing, and life with chronic illnesses just about everywhere *@XannasBooks* or on her website *XannaRenae.com*

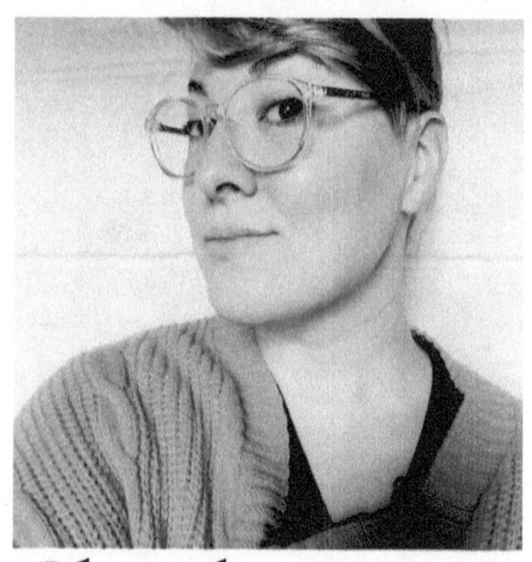

Sheela Kean

Sheela Kean is a Michigan-based author of horror and paranormal suspense. Her previous titles include *Sleep Wakers*, and *Night Frequencies*. Inspired by her late grandmother's book collecting, she is an avid reader of multiple genres and active in the bookish community. She enjoys spending time in Northern Michigan with her husband and children, quilting, and being a full-time geek.

You'll often find her furiously scribbling away in the many notebooks she keeps in her basement office, I wouldn't read them if I were you.

Website: *SheelaKean.com*

Twitter & Instagram: *@SheelaKean*

Kristen Bazen

Kristen Bazen discovered the magic of the written word in elementary school, and she completed her first novella in fifth grade. Now, she mainly writes speculative fiction with a Middle Eastern flavor and strong Christian themes. Every so often, she writes poetry to process life's difficult seasons, and finds that collecting words on a page helps lead her back to the God of hope and light. Two of her poems are featured in the anthology *The Heights We'll Fly To*. When she's not working or writing, Kristen dabbles in languages, trains in martial arts, and raises awareness on how ordinary people can fight human trafficking.

You can find her online at *kristenbazen.com*, or on Instagram as *@kristen_thewriteending*.

Kathryn Reilly

By day, Kathryn helps her students investigate the power of words and master grammar's awesomeness. By night, she reads retold myths, fairy tale mash-ups, and dark adventures when she isn't breathing life into new ones herself. Find her latest poems in *Shadow Atlas: Dark Landscapes of the Americas, Last Girls Club, Whiptail Journal* and *Blink Ink*. She has short stories forthcoming with Tree and Stone, Oddity Prodigy Productions, and Elly Blue Publishing. Her two rescue mutts, Savvie and Roxy Razzamatazz, hear all the stories first. Social: *@Katecanwrite*.

Beka Gremikova

Beka Gremikova writes folkloric fantasy from her little nook in the Ottawa Valley, Ontario, Canada. Some of her first stories were human survival tales featuring animal companions and written on scrap paper her mother brought home from work, complete with her own illustrations. Nowadays, her stories lie in the more fantastical direction, often including twists on familiar archetypes, and she enjoys a soft spot for darkly-whimsical-yet-hopeful tales.

Her work can be found on Havok Publishing's website and in several of their anthologies, as well as other collections, including *Fantasea, Sharper Than Thorns,* and *Tales From the Tower.* Currently, she's plotting a plethora of retellings and plans to release her twisty Cinderella-inspired short story, "The Other Cinderella," in August 2022. You can sign up for her newsletter at *bekagremikova.com.*
Photo Credit: Sarah-Ann Wijngaarden

Cortney Manning

Cortney Manning resides in Florida but has always loved traveling the world. She holds a master's degree in Victorian Literature from the University of Glasgow and has a not-so-secret love of fantasy as well. In her free time, Cortney enjoys walking, drawing, and afternoon tea.

Website: *cortneymanning.wixsite.com/author*

Social Media: *cortneymanningauthor*

Anne J. Hill

Anne J. Hill is an author who enjoys writing fantasy for all ages. Her love of words has also led to her career as a freelance writer and editor. She spends her days dreaming up fantastical realms, talking out loud to the characters in her head, and rearranging her personal library, which has been affectionately dubbed the "Book Dungeon."

Where to find Anne:

annejhill.com

@anne.j.hill.editing

Julia Skinner

Julia Skinner is a nineteen-year-old, modern-day hobbit, with a love for good stories and chocolate ice cream. She lives in South Texas with her family and two miniature Australian Shepherds (and a ton of other animals). When she's not working on one of her many fantasy novels or flash fictions, she can be found juggling college, playing video games, dreaming up yet another entrepreneurial project, or happy-ranting about Brandon Sanderson's books. She is a sinner saved by Jesus, and if any good comes from her journey, it's because of Him.

Her published works include *Prismatic, Fool's Honor, Casting Call, Darkness & Moonlight,* and more! You can join her on her writing journey over on Instagram *@litaflamestories*

Hannah Carter

Hannah Carter is just a girl who loves to dream and write and still wakes up every day hoping to figure out she's secretly a mermaid. As well as her piece included in *The Willow Tree Swing,* her short stories and award-winning flash fiction pieces have also been published in anthologies such as SR Press's *Whispers From Before,* Havok's *Prismatic* and *Casting Call,* Alex Silvius's *The Depths We'll Go To* and *The Heights We'll Fly To,* Effie Joe Stock's *Aphotic Love,* and Anne J. Hill's *Fool's Honor.* Hannah also won a competition with her short story, *Lara.* She currently has two published novellas, *Amir and the Moon* and *Seashells.* In addition to fiction, she also has had over a dozen devotionals published in various magazines, as well as three devotions published in *Finding God in Anime.* In her spare time, she's probably either cuddling her cats, drinking tea, reading, or practicing for her imaginary Broadway debut.

Social Media: @ *introvertedmermaid3*

Willow Whitehead

Willow Whitehead has a love/hate relationship with writing, the words will spill onto the page faster than she can type, or she'll stare at a blank document for hours. Though the words always come a bit easier in the middle of the night. Currently, she spends her days reading, drinking tea, and chasing her black cat, Z, through the woods. You can follow her on Instagram @ *weepingwillowreviews*, and watch as she struggles to balance her time between work, rest, and her innumerable hobbies. The Willow Tree Swing includes her first publication in the world of writing.

Final Thanks

We'd like to thank everyone on the Nightshade Publishing® team for their hard work and dedication to this project—the first multi-author anthology we've published!

We thank every family member, friend, and fan of the authors for picking up a copy of *The Willow Tree Swing*. Without your support, we couldn't do what we do. And your unconditional support of your loved ones allows them to do what they love.

Being an author isn't easy, but it is rewarding.

If you enjoyed this anthology and have made it to this point, we'd love for you to review the collection! Reviews help the life of a book more than you could ever know.

Follow Nightshade Publishing® on their website NightshadePublishing.com and online *@NightshadePublishing*.

www.ingramcontent.com/pod-product-compliance
Lightning Source LLC
Chambersburg PA
CBHW031415310726
48971CB00003B/879